D1135067

– with –

Snack Swap

visit us at
www.abdopublishing.com

Exclusive Spotlight library bound edition published in 2007 by Spotlight, a division of ABDO Publishing Group, Edina, Minnesota. Spotlight produces high quality reinforced library bound editions for schools and libraries. Published by agreement with Archie Comic Publications, Inc.

Library of Congress Cataloging-in-Publication Data

Laugh with snack swap.
    p. cm. -- (The Archie digest library)
    Revision of issue no. 162 (Jan. 2001) of Laugh digest magazine.
    ISBN-13: 978-1-59961-282-9
    ISBN-10: 1-59961-282-8
    1. Graphic Novels. I. Laugh digest magazine. 162. II. Title: Snack swap.

PN6728.A72 L46 2007
741.5'973--dc22

                     2006051234

All Spotlight books are reinforced library binding
and manufactured in the United States of America.

Contents

Laugh

I CAN'T WAIT TO GET TO THE MUSEUM!

YOU MUST BE KIDDING!

Archie & The Gang in FIELD TRIPPED!

SCRIPT: DAN PARENT PENCILS: TIM KENNEDY INKS: RUDY LAPICK
COLORS: FRANK GAGLIARDO LETTERS: BILL YOSHIDA
EDITORS: NELSON RIBEIRO & VICTOR GORELICK EDITOR-IN-CHIEF: RICHARD GOLDWATER

NO! I LOVE CULTURE AND LEARNING!

I'D LEARN PLENTY IF WE'D JUST GO TO THE MALL!

YOU SHOULD BE HAPPY THAT WE'RE OUT OF SCHOOL TODAY!

WELL, YOU'VE GOT A POINT THERE!

I'LL FEEL BETTER IF I JUST GET A BIT OF SHUT-EYE!

LATER... OKAY, CLASS...FINISH UP YOUR LUNCH AND WE'LL GO BACK TO THE BUS AND RETURN HOME!

ATTENTION! WE'RE GOING HOME ON BUS #57, *NOT* THE BUS WE CAME ON!

GULP!

I HOPE VERONICA ISN'T STILL ON OUR OLD BUS!

WELL...SHE'S NOT ON THIS BUS!

MISS GRUNDY, VERONICA WAS ON OUR OLD BUS! SHE WENT OUT THERE TO TAKE A BREAK!

WHERE'S THE BUS WE ARRIVED ON?

IT LEFT TWO HOURS AGO!

214

3

Betty in "COOL RECEPTION"

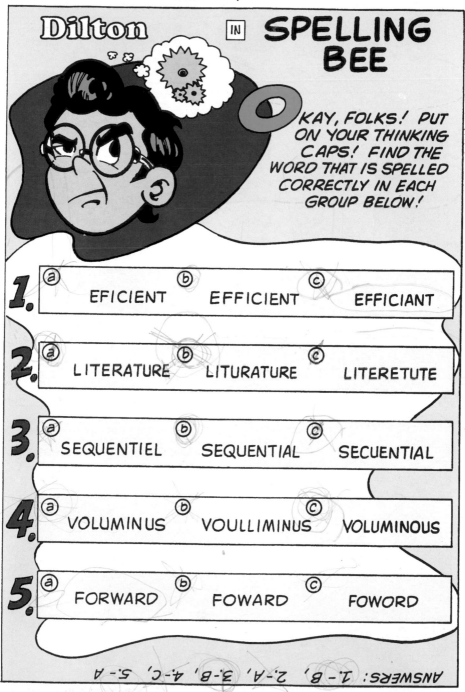

Sabrina HOLi-DAZED & CONFUSED

PART ONE

LET'S SEE IF MY THANKSGIVING DINNER LIST IS *COMPLETE!*

WE'LL HAVE TURKEY BRAINS, BAT GIZZARD STUFFING, EYE OF NEWT PIE!

KA-VOOM!

SABRINA, WHAT *EXACTLY* ARE YOU DOING?

PLANNING MY FESTIVE THANKSGIVING DINNER, DELLA!

THAT'S RIDICULOUS! WE'RE WITCHES! WE *DON'T* CELEBRATE HOLIDAYS! WE *DESTROY* THEM FOR OTHERS!

①

②

"WITCHES AND WARLOCKS WHO'VE GONE *ASTRAY*, BE SENT IN TIME TO ANOTHER HOLIDAY.'"

ZAP!

THERE! ALL SABRINA'S *FRIENDS* AND *RELATIVES* WILL BE SENT *BACK* IN TIME, TO DIFFERENT HOLIDAYS!

I'LL CHANGE THINGS BACK ONCE SABRINA HAS *LEARNED* THE LESSON THAT NOBODY MESSES WITH ME!

SO... IT'S THANKSGIVING! *NONE* OF MY FRIENDS AND FAMILY HAVE SHOWN UP YET! THIS IS SO *STRANGE!*

I'VE *CALLED* EYEDA AND CLEARA, AND THEIR PARENTS *HAVEN'T* SEEN THEM!

--AND AUNT HILDA'S *DISAPPEARED* INTO THIN AIR! I FEEL SOMETHING'S UP!

3

4

ONLY ONE THING TO DO! YOU'LL HAVE TO ZAP BACK TO EACH HOLIDAY TO MAKE SURE DELLA DOESN'T ALTER HISTORY!

CAN YOU GIVE ME A *BOOST?*

YES! I'LL *STAY* HERE IN CASE DELLA STORMS IN!

TA! TA!

BOING!

HERE I AM! THERE'S EYEDA AT THE *FIRST* THANKSGIVING DINNER!

IT LOOKS LIKE SHE'S PREPARING DINNER WITH THEM!

I DON'T KNOW *WHO* I AM OR WHAT I'M DOING HERE, BUT *SOMETHING* TELLS ME CRANBERRY SAUCE WOULD GO WELL WITH THIS!

I'LL JUST *MASH* THE CRANBERRIES UP! TOO BAD THESE WEREN'T ALREADY MASHED UP AND IN A CAN!

WHAT A GREAT *INVENTION* THAT WOULD BE!

MASH!

OKAY, PILGRIMS! OKAY, INDIANS! DINNER IS *SERVED!*

⑤

ALL I KNOW IS I'M AN *INVISIBLE GIRL* WHO'S ICING OVER! THANK GOODNESS FOR MY *INVISIBLE THERMAL UNDIES!*

THAT'S NICE!

CRAK!

AREN'T YOU A LITTLE STARTLED THAT I'M *INVISIBLE?*

SO WHAT? WE'RE *TWO FEET TALL* WITH *POINTY EARS!*

LOOK OUT BELOW!

WE'D BETTER CLEAR THE RUNWAY! THIS LOOKS SERIOUS!

MOO!

WHUMP!

BONK!

MOO!

DARN IT! *COWS* AREN'T GOING TO WORK, EITHER!

EVERYTIME THEY SEE SOMETHING GREEN THEY WANT TO STOP AND GRAZE!

WHAT'S GOING ON?

SANTA'S GOT THE IDEA OF DELIVERING TOYS TO KIDS AROUND THE WORLD *TONIGHT,* IF HE CAN FIND THE RIGHT ANIMALS TO PULL HIS SLEIGH!

10

TRY FEEDING THE REINDEER THIS!

CORN? THEY'RE ALWAYS STEALING IT OUT OF THE GREENHOUSE ANYWAY!

THE CORN PLANTS ARE MAGICAL NOW! I PUT A SPELL ON THEM! IF THE REINDEER EAT THE CORN THEY CAN FLY!

CRUNCH! CRUNCH!

ZIP!

AND SO...

THANKS FOR YOUR HELP, STRANGERS! WE'LL KEEP GROWING THE MAGICAL CORN!

HERE'S A LITTLE TOKEN OF OUR GRATITUDE!

DOLLS! ...OF US! COOL!

MERRY CHRISTMAS! HO! HO! HO!

WE'D BETTER GET GOING, TOO!

ZAP!

NEXT STOP— NEW YEAR'S!

HEE! HEE! THEY HAVE TM-ARCHIE COMIC PUBLICATIONS STAMPED ON OUR BEHINDS!

INVISIBLE & PROUD

CONTINUED (13)

POOF!

SABRINA! I GUESS AUNT HILDA DIDN'T TAKE KINDLY TO YOU EITHER!

SHE REFUSES TO LET THE BABY OUT! AND IF I GO BACK IN SHE'LL JUST *ZAP* ME AGAIN!

HMMM! WE NEED SOME TYPE OF TROJAN HORSE!

THAT'S SILLY!

HOW'S SHE GOING TO GET A *GIANT WOODEN HORSE* IN THE HOUSE? IT'S ONLY A *SPLIT LEVEL RANCH!*

NO, EYEDA! HE MEANS SOMETHING LIKE THIS...

WE HIDE IN SOMETHING SHE CAN'T RESIST, SHE BRINGS IT IN, WE DISTRACT HER AND FATHER TIME GRABS THE BABY!

IT COULD WORK!

KNOCK! KNOCK!

WHO'S THERE?

IT'S A JUMBO DELIVERY OF COLONEL BEELZEBUB'S *FRIED BAT WINGS!*

I'M AFRAID YOU'VE... WHAT AM I SAYING? THAT'S MY *FAVORITE* FOOD!

17

THE END

HOLY TOLEDO! WHAT WAS IN THAT STUPID THING?!!

SOME SORT OF STUFF FLEW OUT OF IT! *WAIT!!* THERE'S A *NAME* ON THE SIDE OF THIS BOX! IT'S... AAARGH!!

PANDORA? I'VE HEARD SOMETHING REAL NASTY ABOUT THAT NAME...

MOM! MOM! I NEED YOU! COME HERE ... AND BRING YOUR COLLEGE EDUCATION WITH YOU!

WHO IS *PANDORA?*

HMMMM... YES... THAT'S A FAMILIAR NAME...

GREEK MYTHOLOGY! ZEUS GOT ANGRY AND ORDERED VULCAN TO CREATE A WOMAN WHOM ALL MEN WOULD DESIRE...

SOUNDS GOOD TO ME!

2

ALL THE GODS GAVE HER GIFTS! KNOWLEDGE, BEAUTY, CUNNING, FLATTERY...

SO WHAT'S WRONG WITH BEING *GIFTED?*

THEY ALSO GAVE HER A BOX... AND WARNED HER *NEVER* TO OPEN IT!

THAT WAS UNFAIR! WHO COULD RESIST SUCH A THING?

YOU'RE RIGHT! SHE *COULDN'T!*

AND ALL THE WORLD'S VICES, SINS, EVILS OF ALL KINDS FLEW OUT! SHE SHUT THE BOX QUICKLY!!

GOLLY!!

ONLY *'HOPE'* WAS LEFT--MANKIND'S COMFORT!

WOW!!

OHMIGOSH! HISTORY REPEATS ITSELF! I LET LOOSE ALL THE WORLD'S EVILS!

③

Ethel in "VACATION DEFLATION"

HI, ETHEL!

HI, BETTY!
HI, RONNIE!

YOU'LL LIKE THE LODGE, BETS!

I HEAR THERE ARE *THREE BOYS UP HERE* FOR *EVERY GIRL!*

SKI VALLEY LODGE

THAT'S STRANGE! I'VE BEEN HERE A WEEK AND I DON'T HAVE A *SINGLE* BOYFRIEND!

HMM!

SKI VALLEY LODGE

OKAY! WHICH ONE OF YOU GIRLS GRABBED MY 3 BOYS?

End

GET SET FOR ANOTHER GREAT STORY WITH ME BACK WHEN I WAS KNOWN AS...
Little Archie

Little Archie in "LESSON LEARNED"

R-RIN-NG-G!

WHY DO I ALWAYS FEEL SO SLEEPY ON SCHOOL DAYS?

LOOK AT ALL THAT SNOW OUTSIDE!

R-RING-G

AND OUR CLASS IS HAVING A BIG SPELLING TEST TODAY!

CLICK!

AND THAT DOESN'T MAKE ME FEEL VERY WELL!

EAT YOUR BREAKFAST, SON, YOU'LL BE LATE FOR SCHOOL!

I-I DON'T FEEL VERY GOOD TODAY!

1

N-NO SCHOOL?

YEAH! PRETTY GOOD, HUH!

WELL, AT LEAST YOU GUYS CAN PLAY A FEW GAMES WITH ME!

THE BOYS CAN'T STAY!

THEIR MOTHERS WOULDN'T WANT THEM AROUND A SICK BOY!

BESIDES, WE'RE ON OUR WAY TO THE MOVIES!

THERE'S AN ALL-CARTOON SHOW AT THE BIJOU!

TOO BAD YOU CAN'T COME WITH US!

ALL CARTOONS?

S'LONG, BOYS, ENJOY THE SHOW!

THANKS, MR. ANDREWS!

JUST A MINUTE, YOUNG MAN, YOU SEEM TO RESEMBLE A BOY I KNOW WHO'S SICK!

YOU CERTAINLY GOT WELL FAST!

A LITTLE REST CAN WORK WONDERS! HEH! HEH!

3

HOT DOG THANKS YOU AND SO DO MY *THUMBS*!

I'LL BRING IT OVER WHEN I'M DONE!

DAYS LATER...

ARF! ARF!

HOT DOG SOUNDS *EXCITED*! I'D BETTER SEE WHAT'S GOING ON!

DILTON! YOU'RE DONE *ALREADY*?

OF COURSE!

SAY HELLO TO THE *21ST CENTURY DOGHOUSE*!

ARF!

IT LOOKS LIKE A GREAT PLACE TO SLEEP!

WAIT TILL YOU SEE WHAT *ELSE* IT DOES!

HOT DOG, SET DOWN YOUR *BONE* IN FRONT OF THE HOUSE!

COOL! IT'S *BURYING* IT FOR HIM!

CHECK OUT THIS NEXT THING!

②